# Katie Woo

# Red, White, and Blue and Katie Woo!

by Fran Manushkin

illustrated by Tammie Lyon

PICTURE WINDOW BOOKS

a capstone imprint

Katie Woo is published by Picture Window Books,
A Capstone Imprint
1710 Roe Crest Drive
North Mankato, MN 56003
www.capstonepub.com

Library of Congress Cataloging-in-Publication Data is
available on the Library of Congress website.
ISBN: 978-1-4048-5985-2 (library binding)
ISBN: 978-1-4048-6364-4 (paperback)

Summary: Katie celebrates the Fourth of July with Pedro and JoJo.

Art Director: Kay Fraser
Graphic Designer: Emily Harris

Photo Credits
Fran Manushkin, pg. 26
Tammie Lyon, pg. 26

# Table of Contents

# Chapter 1
# Katie's Favorite Holiday

"The Fourth of July is my favorite holiday!" said Katie Woo.

JoJo laughed. "Katie, you say that about every holiday!"

"I guess I do," Katie said with a smile. "But the Fourth of July is the best! We're having a parade and a party in my backyard."

"And don't forget the fireworks," said Pedro.

Katie and Pedro and JoJo

put red, white, and blue

decorations on their bikes.

Everyone cheered when

they rode by in the parade.

"Way to go!" yelled Katie's

mom and dad.

## Chapter 2
# Backyard Fun

After the parade, they

went back to Katie's house.

Pedro said, "Katie, your yard

is so big, we can play soccer

in it."

Katie kicked the ball hard.

"I can get it!" yelled

Pedro. He backed up to hit

the ball with his head.

Oops! Pedro tripped over

the table and fell down. He

spilled cherry soda all over

his head!

"No points for you!"

yelled Katie Woo.

"The hot dogs are ready,"
called her dad. "Where are
the buns?"

"Uh-oh!" Katie groaned.

"JoJo's dog ate them!"

The hot dogs looked

lonely without buns.

Katie's mom put out big
bowls of strawberries and
blueberries and whipped
cream.

"We'll eat this later," she
said. "It will be our dessert."

"I'd like to eat

it now," said JoJo.

"Come on,"

Katie said. "Let's

play ringtoss."

The three friends tossed

red, white, and blue hoops at

stakes in the ground.

"I keep missing!" said
JoJo. She cheered herself up
by eating a few blueberries.
Whenever she missed, JoJo
ate some more.

Pedro won the ringtoss
game.

"Uh-oh," JoJo groaned.
"I think I ate too many
blueberries. I have a
stomachache."

## Chapter 3
# Friends and Fireworks

Then it began to rain!

"Oh, no!" Katie groaned.

"No fireworks!"

They began bringing all

the food inside.

Katie carried the
whipped cream.

"I'd like a
little taste," Katie
decided. She pressed
the button hard — too hard!

Whipped cream sprayed
everywhere! JoJo's dog licked
it up.

"Our Fourth of July party

is truly red, white, and blue,"

said Katie. "Pedro turned

red when he spilled cherry

soda on his head. I am white

because I'm covered with

whipped cream."

"And I felt blue," said JoJo, "from eating too many blueberries."

"Look," said Pedro, "the rain stopped."

"Yay!" cheered Katie. "There will be fireworks!"

"First, let's have dessert,"

said Katie's mom.

"I'll skip the blueberries,"

decided JoJo.

The three friends sat together in the backyard.

"What color will the fireworks be?" asked Pedro.

"Red, white, and blue!" said Katie.

And she was right.

## About the Author

Fran Manushkin is the author of many popular picture books, including *How Mama Brought the Spring; Baby, Come Out!; Latkes and Applesauce: A Hanukkah Story;* and *The Tushy Book.* There is a real Katie Woo — she's Fran's great-niece — but she never gets in half the trouble of the Katie Woo in the books. Fran writes on her beloved Mac computer in New York City, without the help of her two naughty cats, Cookie and Goldy.

## About the Illustrator

Tammie Lyon began her love for drawing at a young age while sitting at the kitchen table with her dad. She continued her love of art and eventually attended the Columbus College of Art and Design, where she earned a bachelors degree in fine art. After a brief career as a professional ballet dancer, she decided to devote herself full time to illustration. Today she lives with her husband, Lee, in Cincinnati, Ohio. Her dogs, Gus and Dudley, keep her company as she works in her studio.

# Glossary

**cheered** (CHEERD)—shouted praise to let people know that something is liked

**decorations** (dek-uh-RAY-shuhns)—things added to make something prettier

**dessert** (di-ZURT)—a sweet food served at the end of a meal

**favorite** (FAY-vuh-rit)—the thing you like best

**groaned** (GROHND)—made a long, low sound to show unhappiness

**stomachache** (STUHM-uhk-ake)—a dull pain in the stomach that goes on and on

**whenever** (wen-EV-er)—at every time

**whipped cream** (WIPT KREEM)—cream that has been beat into a foam

# Discussion Questions

1. How do you celebrate the Fourth of July? Do you have any traditions that you do every year?

2. Have you ever been in a parade? Have you ever watched a parade? Describe what you saw.

3. What do you think was Katie's favorite part of her day? Which part would you like the best?

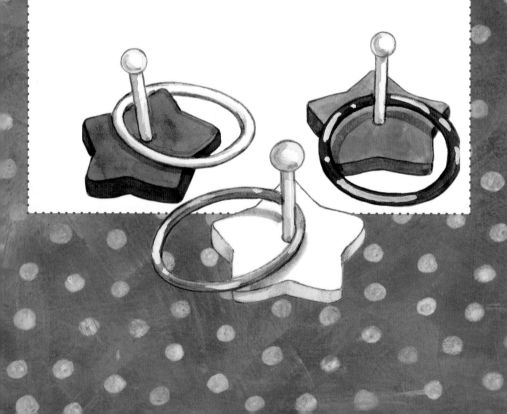

# Writing Prompts

1. Write down three facts you know about the Fourth of July. If you can't think of three, ask a grown-up to help you find some in a book or on the computer.

2. The Fourth of July is America's birthday. Make a birthday card for the country. Be sure to write a special message.

3. Katie and her friends ate lots of yummy food on the Fourth of July. Draw a picture of your favorite summer food. Then write a sentence that explains what you like about it.

# Cooking with Katie

People love to serve berries on the Fourth of July. They are sweet and delicious. Plus, they are the perfect color to celebrate the day.

With this recipe, you can make your berries into a star, and show your American pride.

Before you start, ask a grown-up for help. And don't forget to wash your hands!

## Super Star-berry Dessert
*Makes 1

Ingredients:
- 5 strawberries
- whipped cream cheese
- 5 blueberries

Other things you need:
- a plate
- a butter knife

**What you do:**

1. Wash the berries. Ask a grown-up to help you remove the green leaf and white flesh at the top of the strawberries. This is called hulling the strawberries.

2. Spread the top of each strawberry with about a tablespoon of whipped cream cheese.

3. Place a blueberry on top of the cream cheese.

4. Arrange the berries in a star shape on your plate. The blueberries should point inward, and the bottoms of the strawberries should point outward to make the tips of the star.